TOYLAND TALES

By V. Gilbert Beers

Illustrated by Helen Endres

MOODY PRESS • CHICAGO

What You Will Find in This Book

© 1984 by V. Gilbert Beers

ISBN: 0-8024-9574-5

Printed in the United States of America

Moody Press, a ministry of the Moody Bible Institute, is designed for education, evangelization, and edification. If we may assist you in knowing more about Christ and the Christian life, please write us without obligation: Moody Press, c/o MLM, Chicago, Illinois 60610.

TO PARENTS AND TEACHERS

Have you ever visited Toyland? Surely you must have gone there in your imagination. Almost every child dreams of going to be with Jack-in-the-Box, a doll, Nutcracker, a windup mouse, and of course wooden soldiers.

This is a book that bridges the real world and the world of fantasy, where real children can walk and talk among their toys. It also bridges the world of fiction and truth, where Bible truth and the fictitious Muffin Family characters come together.

The popular members of the Muffin Family are role models of Christian truth. The way they solve their problems shows how people everywhere should live out Bible truth in daily living.

Toyland Tales is the twelfth in the Muffin Family Picture Bible series. Other volumes are *Through Golden Windows, Under the Tagalong Tree, With Sails to the Wind, Over Buttonwood Bridge, From Castles in the Clouds, With Maxi and Mini in Muffkinland, Out of the Treasure Chest, Along Thimblelane Trails, Treehouse Tales, Muffkins on Parade,* and *Captain Maxi's Secret Island.*

A Time to Say Hello

Please Listen
Genesis 25:20-26

Why isn't God listening? Isaac and Rebekah must have wondered.

Their friends had babies. Their neighbors had babies. But they did not have even one baby.

Isaac and Rebekah had been married twenty years. That's a long time to be married and still have no baby.

Each day Isaac and Rebekah watched the neighbor children. Some of the little girls and boys played around their tents. The older boys helped their fathers with the chores, taking care of the sheep and goats. The older girls helped their mothers churn butter or fix the family clothes.

Isaac and Rebekah were sad when they saw those boys and girls. The boys and girls looked so happy. That made the mothers and fathers happy too. And that made Isaac and Rebekah want a baby even more. That's why they were sad.

Each day Isaac and Rebekah talked to God about a baby. "Please give us a baby," they prayed. But God did not give them a baby.

Why isn't God listening? Isaac and Rebekah must have wondered. "Why doesn't God give us a baby?"

Of course God was listening, even though He did not give them a baby for a long time. He was listening and waiting for the right time.

Then one day Isaac and Rebekah had twin baby boys. Don't you think they were surprised?

The first baby boy was red and had hair all over him. They named him *Esau.* Some say that meant "red." Others say it meant "hairy." Since Esau was both red and hairy, perhaps it meant both.

The second baby was born soon after the first. He was born so soon after Esau that he grabbed Esau's heel as they were born.

7

Isaac and Rebekah named this second boy *Jacob*. That meant "he grabs the heel." People sometimes named children after things like that.

Now Isaac and Rebekah knew that God had been listening to them each time they prayed. He had heard their prayers. But God had waited until just the right time to answer. We should remember that when we think God is not listening to us.

WHAT DO YOU THINK?
What this story teaches: When you pray, God listens to you. He gives you what you need. Sometimes He does not give you what you want. And sometimes He lets you wait for the answer.
1. What did Isaac and Rebekah want more than anything else? Whom did they ask to help them?
2. Did God give them a baby as soon as they asked? How did He answer their prayer?
3. Did God answer yes, no, or wait? What do you think Isaac and Rebekah said to God when their baby boys were born? What should we say when God gives us something special?

8

Stop, Go, Maybe So

A Muffin Family Story

"Poppi, why doesn't God give me a new bike?" Mini asked.

Poppi looked up from the toy cars that he and Maxi had lined up on the floor. He looked surprised at Mini's question.

Mini kept on talking. "I have asked God for a bike every night this week, but He just doesn't listen to me," Mini said.

"Do you mean He doesn't hear you or doesn't give you what you want?" Poppi asked.

Mini thought for a minute. "He must hear me," she said. "I know God hears me. But He doesn't answer."

"Perhaps He did answer," said Poppi. "But He didn't answer the way you thought He should."

Mini looked puzzled.

"Watch this toy car," said Poppi. Poppi pushed a toy car up to a little toy stoplight. It had a red, green, and yellow light on it, just like a real stoplight downtown.

"The light is red," said Poppi. "What should my car do?"

Mini knew the answer to that one. She had watched Poppi many times when they had come up to a red light in their real car.

"Stop!" said Mini.

"Now the light is yellow," said Poppi. "What should I do?"

"Go!" said Maxi, without waiting for Mini to answer.

"Not yet," said Poppi. "Not until it changes to another color. Yellow means 'wait just a little longer until the green light says go,' or 'get ready to go.' "

"Does it always mean that?" asked Mini.

"Not always," said Poppi. "Suppose you are driving along the street and the light is green. Suddenly the yellow light comes on. What do you think that means?"

"Slow down, get ready to stop," said Mini.

"Good," said Poppi. "Now what does the green light mean?"

"GO!" said Maxi. This time Maxi was right.

"But what does that have to do with praying for a bike?" asked Mini.

"Let's pretend God is going to answer your prayer with this stoplight," said Poppi. "You have just finished praying for your bike. Now God turns on the green light. What do you think He is saying?"

Mini thought for a minute. "I think He is saying yes, He will give me a bike," said Mini.

"I think so, too," said Poppi. "So He answered your prayer, right?"

"Right," said Mini.

"But suppose He turned on the red light instead," said Poppi. "What is He saying?"

"He won't let Mini have her bike," said Maxi. "He is saying no." Mini nodded her head. She thought Maxi was right.

"But did He answer you?" asked Poppi.

"I . . . I guess so," said Mini. "He said no."

"Now what if God had turned on the yellow light?" said Poppi. "What is He saying?"

Maxi and Mini looked at each other. They weren't sure. God wasn't saying no. He wasn't saying yes.

"Could God be saying maybe, or wait?" asked Poppi. "But He still answered, didn't He?"

Mini smiled. "I wish God could turn on lights like that," she said. "Then I would know what He is saying."

"But He doesn't do it that way," said Poppi.

"I know," said Mini. "But I am glad to know that God is listening and that He is answering with a red, yellow, or green."

"By the way, your light is green," said Maxi. "You can drive your car on now."

Poppi, Maxi, and Mini all laughed as Poppi drove his toy car on, with Maxi's car following.

LET'S TALK ABOUT THIS

What this story teaches: God answers every prayer. Sometimes He says yes, sometimes no, and sometimes He says wait, or maybe so.

1. Have you been praying for something lately?

2. What did you learn about the way God answers prayer?

3. Do you remember to thank God when He answers?

A Boy with Two Names

Genesis 35:16-20

Jacob and Rachel should have been happy. They were going to have a new baby.

But it is hard to have a baby on a long trip. Jacob and his family had to go far away. They were going to a new home in another land.

All day long Rachel rode on her camel. The camel plopped up and down. It swayed from side to side. Who wants to ride like that all day? It isn't easy when a lady is going to have a baby. But what could Rachel do? What could Jacob do? They had to go to the new land.

"I wish we were in our new home," Jacob must have told Rachel many times. But they weren't. So they had to keep on going.

Jacob and his family went on and on for many days. Jacob could see how tired Rachel was. But where could they stop? There was no good place to stay.

At last Jacob and his family came to Bethlehem. That was not their new home. But they had to stop anyway. Rachel was ready to have her baby.

Then something went wrong. Things were not going the way they should.

Rachel grew worse. The lady who was helping her did not know what to do. People then did not have good doctors or hospitals to help at a time like that. So they had to do the best they could.

At last Rachel's new baby was born. "You have a baby boy," Rachel's helper told her.

Rachel was so tired and weak she could hardly answer. But at last she said, "We will name him *Ben-Oni*." Then Rachel died.

13

Jacob did not like his new son's name. It meant "son of my trouble." Jacob did not want his son to be called "son of my trouble" all his life. So Jacob gave his son a new name, *Benjamin*. That meant "son of my right hand." Jacob was calling his son a special helper. That really was a better name, wasn't it?

Our names are important. Nobody wants to live with a name that means "trouble." But "helper" is a good name. Which name would you rather have?

WHAT DO YOU THINK?
What this story teaches: What we call each other is important. Shouldn't we call each other good names instead of bad ones?
1. What was Benjamin's name at first? What did it mean?
2. Why did Jacob change that first name? What new name did he give him? Which do you like better?
3. What names do others call you? Which do you like? Which do you not like? Why?
4. The name *Christian* means "like Jesus." Would you like to be like Jesus? Would you like to be called "Christian"? You are a Christian when you accept Jesus as your Savior. Would you like to do that now?

Come to the Great Puppet Show

A Muffin Family Story

"Come one, come all," Maxi called out, trying to sound important. "Come to the greatest puppet show on earth."

Pookie, BoBo, Charlie, Maria, and Tony shuffled their chairs. Maxi tapped his hand on the Muffin Family Puppet Theater until all his friends sat down.

Mini straightened the strings on the puppets, and the show was ready to begin. "Welcome to the Muffin Family Puppet Theater," said Maxi. "We're ready to go when you are."

"Before you start, kid, I'd like to know where you got the name *Muffin*," said BoBo, trying to be funny.

Maxi was surprised. He wasn't sure what to answer.

"Aw, he got it down at the bakery," Pookie chimed in.

"Speaking of names," said Charlie. "Who ever hung the names *Pookie* and *BoBo* on you guys?" Charlie was trying to help Maxi.

"What about *CHARRR-lee*?" Tony snapped. "That's not the hottest name around either."

Marie stamped her foot. "Shame on all you dumb guys for calling each other names," she shouted.

"Maria!" said Mini. "Now you're calling them a bad name."

Before long, bad names were flying back and forth. Suddenly the great puppet show was over.

Pookie left without saying good-by. BoBo said he would never come back to this place. And Tony said he didn't care about puppet shows anyway.

Maria and Mini ran after Pookie, BoBo, and Tony telling them how they should be ashamed of the things they had said.

Maxi sat down by the Muffin Family Puppet Theater. He looked sad sitting there with his head down.

"I'm sorry, Maxi," said Charlie. "I want to be your friend."

Maxi looked up. He smiled. "Do you know what a wonderful name that is?" he asked Charlie.

"What name?" Charlie asked, looking surprised.

"*Friend*," said Maxi. "It's so much better than all the bad names we were calling each other."

"Yeah, I guess it is," said Charlie.

"So let's go find Pookie, BoBo, and Tony and tell them we're their friends, even though they did call us bad names," said Maxi.

Maxi and Charlie started to run from the yard. But they almost bumped into Pookie, BoBo, and Tony coming this way.

"We're glad we found you," said Pookie.

"We want to tell you that we're your friends," said BoBo.

"And we're sorry we called you some bad names," said Tony.

"We were coming to find you," said Charlie.

"To tell you that we're friends, too," said Maxi.

Mini and Maria smiled. "OK, everyone back to the Muffin Family Puppet Theater," said Maria. "This time Mini and I will give the show."

"What's it about?" asked Charlie.

"Some friends who called each other bad names," said Maria. "Then they found it was much better to call each other good names instead."

"Sounds like a great show," said Pookie.

"Let's go see it," said BoBo.

Wouldn't you like to see it, too?

LET'S TALK ABOUT THIS

What this story teaches: Good names are much better than bad names.

1. What happened when the friends started calling each other bad names? Why?

2. Do you and your friends ever call each other bad names? Are you happier when you call each other good names?

3. Which pleases Jesus more, when you and your friends call each other bad names or good names? What are some good names He would like you to call each other?

Look What We Found

What Did You Find?

2 Kings 22; 2 Chronicles 34:1-28

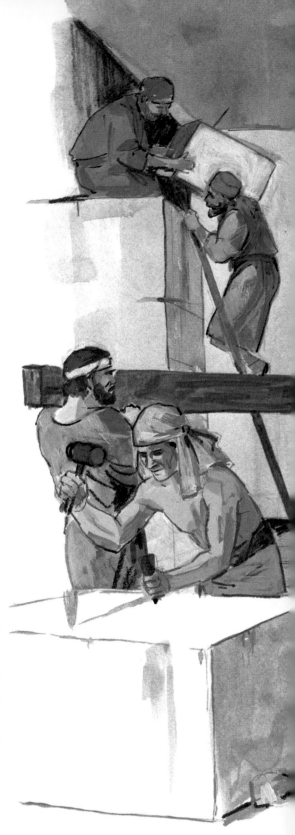

"Fix God's house!" King Josiah commanded. "Pay the workers with the money the people gave."

People ran to do what the king said. When a king said, "Do this," everyone did it. Who wants a king to get angry at him?

Hilkiah the priest was in charge of fixing God's house. What a lot of fixing it needed, too. The people before Hilkiah's time did not take care of God's house. They did not keep it clean or fix it when something went wrong. What a mess! Hilkiah must have been ashamed of it. Now he was glad that King Josiah wanted to fix it.

Hilkiah was glad too that people had given money to fix God's house. This was not the king's money. It was not Hilkiah's money. It was money the people had given. They wanted someone to fix God's house. Then they could talk to God there.

Hilkiah gave orders. "Bring wood!" Some men brought wood. "Bring stones!" Some men brought stones. They hammered and sawed. They laid up stones where they should go. They swept dirt from the corners and tore out bad wood. They put new wood and stone where those things should go.

Each time someone did some work. Hilkiah took money from the big moneychest and paid him. Each day he took more money from the chest.

One day Hilkiah was moving some things in God's house. He saw something strange.

Hilkiah reached out and touched it. He took it into his hands and looked at it carefully. What was it? Then Hilkiah saw that it was an old scroll, buried in some dust and things.

Hilkiah was excited. "This is God's Word!" he whispered. "It is the Book with God's rules in it."

"Look! I have found God's Word!" Hilkiah told one of the king's officers. The officer was excited too. He ran to show it to the king. Then he read some of the Book to the king.

What do you suppose King Josiah thought? He heard God's Word for the first time. He heard what God wanted His people to do.

But now the king was sad. He knew that he and his people had not done what God said in His Book. He knew they could be in trouble with God.

"We and our ancestors have not done what God told us to do," the king said. "We have not obeyed Him. What will God do to us now?"

The king's officers talked with Hulda. She knew much about God. God told her what to say to them.

"The people will be punished," said Hulda. "But this will not happen while Josiah is king. That is because he really does want to please God."

The king was sorry to hear that his people would be punished. But he was glad that it would not be for a while.

WHAT DO YOU THINK?

What this story teaches: If we don't obey when we should, we may get into trouble.

1. What did Hilkiah the priest find in the Temple? Why was he glad to find it?

2. What did he and the king's officers do with this scroll? What did the king say about it?

3. What trouble would the people get into because they had not obeyed God? Why would that not happen while Josiah was king?

Look at That Inside Out, Upside Down Wagon

A Muffin Family Story

"What are you doing, Tony?" Maxi asked.

"Putting my new red wagon together," said Tony. "I got it for my birthday."

"Do you have something that tells how to put it together?" asked Mini.

"Sure, there is a sheet of instructions," said Tony. "But who needs it?"

Maxi looked at Mini. Mini looked at Maxi.

"I wouldn't try to put a red wagon together without reading the instructions," said Mini.

"Me neither," said Maxi. "I'd just get into trouble."

"That's because you're not me," Tony bragged.

"Well, see you later, Tony," said Maxi. Then he and Mini ran down the street to play with Charlie.

"Guess what Tony is doing?" said Mini. "He's putting his new red wagon together."

"Without reading the instructions," said Maxi.

"Oh, wow," said Charlie. "Is he ever headed for trouble."

"That's what we told him," said Maxi. "But he said he didn't need the instructions. Sounds like he knows more than the people who made it."

Charlie laughed. Then he and Mini and Maxi ran down the street to find Pookie.

"Guess what Tony is doing?" Charlie asked Pookie. "He's putting his new red wagon together."

"Without reading the instructions," said Maxi.

"I'd sure get into trouble doing that," said Pookie.

"That's what I told him," said Maxi. "But he says that's because I'm not him. Sounds like he knows more than the people who made it."

Pookie laughed. Then he and Mini and Maxi and Charlie ran down the street to find Maria.

"Guess what Tony is doing," Pookie said to Maria. "He's putting his new red wagon together."

"Without reading the instructions," said Maxie.

"Trouble, trouble, trouble," said Maria. "That's what he's going to get."

"That's what I told him," said Maxi. "But he thinks he knows more than the people who made it."

"Well, let's all go over to Tony's house," said Maria. "We should see what's happening."

So Maria, Pookie, Charlie, Mini, and Maxi ran up the street to Tony's house. Guess what they found. There was Tony, sitting in his red wagon. But he did not look very happy.

"Wow, look at those wheels," said Charlie. "They're inside out."

"And look at the handle," said Pookie. "It's upside down."

"That's the nicest inside out, upside down wagon I've ever seen," said Maria.

Maxi said nothing. He picked up the instruction sheet and handed it to Tony. "This is one thing that's right," said Maxi.

"Yeah, I know," said Tony. "I guess I thought I was smarter than the people who made it. Now come on, you guys. Help me read this stuff, and let's get the wagon together right." So they did.

LET'S TALK ABOUT THIS
What this story teaches: If we don't obey the maker's instructions, we may get into trouble.
1. Who made the red wagon? Did Tony? Who knew more about it, the maker or Tony?
2. Who made you? Who knows more about you than you do?
3. Why should you listen to God's instruction Book, the Bible? Why not do things your way?

What Do You Hear

2 Kings 23:1-3; 2 Chronicles 34:29-33

"Bring all the leaders of our nation here," King Josiah commanded.

The king's men hurried to obey. People always hurried to obey a king. Don't you think you would, too?

Soon the leaders began to come from all parts of the nation. They came to God's house, as the king had told them to do.

The people became quiet as the king began to speak to them. He told them how the priest Hilkiah had found a scroll. It was God's Word. It told what God wanted the people to do. Of course Hilkiah had been excited when he found it.

King Josiah told the people that Hilkiah had given the scroll to one of the king's officers. The officer had read it to the king.

The leaders must have been sad when the king said that God would punish them for not obeying His Word. That would not happen soon, but it would happen.

Then the king began to read God's Word to the leaders. He read all that the scroll said, from beginning to end.

Now the people knew what they should do to please God. They knew why they would be punished.

Then the king did something that not many kings would do. He told all the people that he wanted to live for God. He wanted to do the things that would please God. That was a very brave thing to do, even for a king, wasn't it?

The king promised God that He would obey Him and follow His rules in the scroll. He also asked the people to obey those rules, too.

Then the king ordered some men to break down the evil statues and idols. He wanted his people to obey God and not to worship statues.

Do you think God was pleased to see the king do all those good things He had put in His scroll?

WHAT DO YOU THINK?

What this story teaches: When we know what we should do, we had better do it.

1. Why did the king tell his leaders to meet him at God's house? What did he want to do there?

2. What did the king tell the leaders he wanted to do for God? What did he promise God that day before these leaders?

3. What did the king ask his people to do? What did he do about the evil statues that people worshiped?

4. What do you think God thought about King Josiah? Do you think God was pleased with what he did?

That Stubborn Jack-in-the Box

A Muffin Make-believe Story

Do you like a jack-in-the-box? Just about everyone does. Even the other toys in Toyland liked to be with Jack. When a toy soldier turned Jack's handle, he always popped out with a big smile on his face. When Nutcracker turned Jack's handle, he popped out with a big smile on his face for him, too.

Jack was so much fun that the other toys came all day long. They turned his handle and laughed when he popped out. Then they turned it again and laughed some more when he popped out.

Jack tried to keep smiling. But it is hard to pop out with a big smile all the time.

At last Jack got tired of popping out and smiling at the other toys. So when one toy soldier turned the handle, Jack stayed inside. Nutcracker tried, but Jack still stayed inside. Some of the other toys tried, but no matter how many times they turned the handle, Jack stayed inside.

"That stubborn jack-in-the-box," some of them said. "He's supposed to jump out and smile at us. That's what he was made to do. But Jack still would not come out.

The other toys held a meeting. They tried to think of some way to get Jack out of his box.

"He won't be happy staying in there very long," some said. "Toys have to do what they are made to do. If they don't, how can they be happy?"

That's even true for boys and girls and mommis and poppis, too!

The toys brought Jack's best friends. They turned the handle and asked Jack to come out with his big smile. But he would not do it.

Nutcracker did not like that. He began to pound on Jack's box. He rattled it and shook it and beat on it with his wooden hands. But Jack still would not come out.

"Let's ask the king to come," someone suggested. "He will command Jack to come out. Then he will have to do it. Who would not do what the king tells him to do?"

It was a great idea. Someone sent a message to the king. "Please come and command Jack to come out of his box," they said. "He won't do it for us."

Before long the king came riding upon his little hobbyhorse. All the wooden soldiers lined up. They stood straight and tall as the king rode before them.

Horns tooted. Drums went rat-a-tat-tat-tat. And the toy soldiers saluted. That's what you're supposed to do when a king goes by.

The king rode up to the jack-in-the-box. Everyone in Toyland became quiet as the king ordered someone to turn Jack's handle. Then the king called out to Jack.

"Come out with a big smile!" said the king.

When Jack heard that, he knew it was the king. He would not come out for the toy soldiers. He would not come for Nutcracker. But he popped out with his biggest smile for his king. That's because he wanted to obey the king.

Jack knew what he should do. He should obey his king. And he did it. Don't you think we should obey God and our parents when they tell us to do something?

LET'S TALK ABOUT THIS

What this story teaches: Is there someone you should obey? Don't you think it's good to do it?

1. Why did Jack refuse to come out of his box?

2. Why did the king come? Why do you think Jack came out of his box for the king?

3. Think of some people you should obey. Why should you obey each one?

31

When We Must Say Good-by

Something for a Special Someone

Genesis 23

News spread fast through camp. Everyone who heard it felt sad.

"Sarah? When did she die?"

"Were you there? What happened?"

"When can we see the family?"

"Sarah? Can it be that she is gone? What will poor Abraham do now?"

What would Abraham do now? What could he do now? First he must find a place to bury Sarah. He had loved Sarah very much. So this must be a special place.

Abraham did not own any land. He was a shepherd who moved about from place to place, living in tents. He never settled down and built a house. He never needed to buy land where he could live and plant a vineyard. But now he needed some land where he could bury his wife.

Some of Abraham's neighbors were called Hittites. They owned much of the land around there. One, a man named Ephron, owned a large cave, just what Abraham needed.

When Abraham's neighbors came to see him, they told him how sorry they were. And what could they do to help him?

"Please sell me a place where I can bury Sarah," Abraham told them.

"Of course," said the men. "You are like a prince to us. Choose the best place, and we will sell it to you. What would you like?"

"The cave that belongs to Ephron," Abraham answered.

Ephron was sitting there with the others. He had heard everything that was said.

"I will give you my cave," Ephron said to Abraham.

Ephron did not really want to give his cave away. But that was the way people sold things in those days. Someone would say the other person could have something for nothing. Then the other person would argue that he must pay. Then the person selling it would probably charge much more than it was worth.

"No, I want to buy the cave," Abraham argued. "How much do you want for it?"

Ephron must have smiled when he heard that. Now he could charge Abraham whatever he wanted. He knew Abraham wanted this cave very much. He knew Abraham wanted a special place for Sarah.

Ephron tried to look as if the price was not important. "It's worth four hundred pieces of silver," he said. "But what is that between friends?"

It was a lot of money. It was probably much too much money for that cave. A person could have bought twenty slaves for that price.

But it did not matter to Abraham now. He wanted that special place for the person he had loved most. He would have paid almost anything to get the best for Sarah.

Abraham weighed the silver on some scales. People did not have money then. They had to use silver and gold pieces for money.

The cave belonged to Abraham now. He had probably paid too much. But he had a special place for her.

Sadly Abraham and his friends took Sarah to the cave and buried her. Then they went home. He was sad without Sarah. But he was glad he had found a special place to bury her.

WHAT DO YOU THINK?
What this story teaches: We do special things for special people, don't we?
1. Why did Abraham want a special place to bury Sarah? Do you think Ephron charged too much?
2. What did you learn about Abraham?

Will You Come to My Special Party?

A Muffin Make-believe Story

"What should I do? What should I do?" the king of Toyland asked. The king rocked back and forth on his little hobbyhorse.

"What do you want to do?" asked a wooden soldier who was guarding the king.

"I want to do something special for someone special," said the king.

"Then you must find who is special before you can decide what special thing to do for that special person," said the wooden soldier.

"Oh, thank you, thank you," said the king. "I'm glad that I thought of that. But how do I find someone special?"

"I will ask the other toys in Toyland," said the wooden soldier. "Then I will tell you what they say."

So the king sent the wooden soldier out to ask the other toys.

"Who is the most special person in Toyland?" the wooden soldier asked Nutcracker. The nutcracker thought for a while. "I am," he said at last, "I can crack a nut better than anyone else in Toyland."

When the wooden soldier told the king about Nutcracker, the king thought for a while. "No, he is not the most special person. Look again."

The wooden soldier asked the big drum next. "Who is the most special person in Toyland?"

"I am," said the drum. "Who else can go *boom, boom, boom* and make the soldiers march in time in a parade?"

But the king did not think the drum was the most special person either.

Next the wooden soldier asked the china doll. "I am," said the china doll. "Can you think of anyone in Toyland more beautiful than I?"

The soldier could not think of anyone more beautiful than the china doll. But when he told the king, he shook his head. "No," said the king, "she is not the one."

The soldier went next to see the jack-in-the-box. Jack jumped higher than he had ever jumped and smiled his biggest smile. "Who else?" asked Jack. "Can anyone else in Toyland do that?"

Of course no one else could do that. Not even the king. But when the soldier told the king, he shook his head again. "No," said the king, "he is not the one."

The king rocked back and forth on his hobbyhorse. He thought for a long time. Then he looked at the wooden soldier.

"Who do you think is the most special person?" he asked.

"Oh, you are," said the wooden soldier. "That's why I like to be your helper."

The king jumped from his hobbyhorse. "Hooray!" he shouted. "Now we're ready to have a big party for someone special."

"For you?" asked the wooden soldier.

"No, for you!" said the king. "You are special because you thought someone else was special. And because you really like to be a helper."

Wouldn't you like to go to the king's big party?

LET'S TALK ABOUT THIS

What this story teaches: People are special when they think others are special, not themselves, and when they want to be good helpers.

1. Why were Nutcracker, the drum, the china doll, and Jack not the most special persons to the king?

2. Why was the wooden soldier more special? How would you like to be like him?

How Can I Help You?

Genesis 47:28—50:14

What should a person do when he knows he will die soon? That's what Jacob had to decide. He was old and sick. He knew he would die soon. But before he died he wanted to see his family. He wanted to talk to them.

Jacob asked Joseph to come first. Joseph had always been Jacob's favorite son. Joseph always tried to please his father. And he always tried to please God. No wonder Jacob loved him so much.

"Promise me something," said Jacob. "Take me back to my homeland when I die. Bury me there in the land where I lived before I came here to Egypt."

Joseph promised. Then Jacob asked Joseph to bring his two sons to see him. Some day they would be fathers and leaders among the people. Jacob wanted them to be sure to do what God wanted. He wanted them to please God in all that they did. So he asked God to bless them and help them.

Then once more Jacob asked his family members to come to see him. This time he asked all of his sons to come. They were grown men now. Jacob wanted each of them to please God. He asked God to bless them and help them do their best for Him.

At last Jacob died. Joseph kept his promise. He took Jacob's body back to the land from which he had come. There he buried his father in the cave where Abraham had buried Sarah.

As the years passed, Jacob's sons had many children. Those children had many children and grandchildren. They called themselves Israelites because *Israel* was Jacob's other name. They were proud to be called by Jacob's name. They knew that God loved Jacob, or Israel. And they knew that Jacob loved God.

That's a good way to remember a grandfather, isn't it?

WHAT DO YOU THINK?
What this story teaches: Grandfathers and grandchildren should help each other know God better. So should parents and children, and others in a family.
1. Why were the Israelites proud to be in Jacob's family? What kind of person was he? How do you know that he loved God?
2. Who did Jacob want to talk to before he died? Why did he want to do that?
3. Why is it good to learn about God while we are children? Who should help us learn about Him?
4. Why is it good for us to help others in our families know about God?

A Help-One-Another Family

A Muffin Family Story

"Mommi."

"Yes, Mini."

"Why are dolls usually babies or little girls?"

"So you can hold them and take care of them, Mini. Little girls like to take care of babies."

"Is that because we want to be little mommis?"

"I suppose it is."

"I suppose so, too. But mommis take care of other people, too, don't they?"

"Oh, yes, Mini. Mommis take care of big girls like you."

"And big boys like Maxi?"

"Of course, Mini. We even take care of poppis, like your poppi."

"And Poppi takes care of you, too, doesn't he, Mommi?"

"He certainly does, Mini. He's a wonderful poppi. He takes good care of me. And he takes good care of you, too."

43

"And Maxi?"

"And Maxi."

"Do you and Poppi take care of anyone else?"

"Sometimes we help Grandmommi and Grandpoppi. Sometimes we do things for them that are hard for them to do."

"Do they ever take care of you?"

"Of course. They do good things for us that we can't do as well ourselves."

"And they do many good things for Maxi and me, too. They're a wonderful grandmommi and grandpoppi, aren't they?"

"They're also a wonderful mommi and poppi, Mini. Grandmommi is my mommi. And Grandpoppi is my poppi. Long ago I was their little girl, just as you are my little girl."

"But I'm a big girl."

"Of course you are, Mini. I forgot. I'm sorry. Mommis and poppis sometimes forget that their little girls have grown up to be big girls like you."

"Do Grandmommi and Grandpoppi still think you're their little girl?"

"Sometimes. But then they remember."

"Mommi, what's the most special thing they ever did for you?"

"Mini, they helped me accept Jesus as my Savior. They taught me to love God's Word, the Bible."

"Just like you and Poppi have done for Maxi and me."

"And don't forget, Mini. Grandmommi and Grandpoppi have helped you love God and the Bible too."

44

"Mommi."

"Yes, Mini."

"Do Minis and Maxis ever help mommis and poppis?"

"Of course, Mini. You and Maxi do many good things for Poppi and me."

"Do we ever help you love God more?"

"Yes, you have helped us love God much more. And we have learned much more about God's Word because you are part of our family."

"Do you think Grandmommi and Grandpoppi love God more because of us?"

"Yes, Mini. They have told me so."

"Then we all help each other know God better, don't we?"

"That's the way it should be, Mini."

"I'm glad we're a help-one-another family. But I have to help Ruff and Tuff now by feeding them. 'By, Mommi."

" 'By, Mini."

LET'S TALK ABOUT THIS

What this story teaches: Grandparents and grandchildren should help each other know God better. So should parents and children, and others in a family.

1. Who helps each other in Maxi and Mini's family? Why do you think they do that?

2. What can you do to help others in your family love God more? What can you do to help them know God's Word better?

God's Way or My Way?

Deuteronomy 32:48-52; 34

"You will see the Promised Land," God told Moses. "But you cannot go in."

Moses felt sad when God told him that. He had led his people through the wilderness. They had been there forty years. Now it was time to go into the Promised Land. Moses wanted to go in with his people. But he couldn't.

"You disobeyed Me," God told Moses. "That's why you cannot go in."

That was true. One time God told Moses to speak to a rock so that it would give water for the people. But Moses did not speak to it. Instead, he hit the rock. Perhaps he thought that would make him look more important. But God did not like it. That's why God said he could not go into the Promised Land.

Moses and his people had done many things together. He had led them out of Egypt. He had helped them go across the Red Sea. He had taught them God's rules at Mount Sinai. And he had helped them build God's tent house, the Tabernacle. He had led them everywhere they went.

Now Moses was very sad. More than anything else, he wanted to go into the Promised Land. He wanted to live there with his people. After all those years of camping in the wilderness, Moses wanted to plant a garden and vineyard. He wanted to settle down and build a house.

"You must go up to the top of that mountain," God told Moses. "You will die there."

What could Moses do? He couldn't argue with God. He couldn't run away and hide. God had said he would die in that mountain. So that's what would happen.

Poor Moses! Now he wished he had obeyed God. Now he wished he had spoken to the rock as God told him to do. But he hadn't.

47

People expect their leaders to do what is right, don't they? If their leaders don't, the people will probably not do what is right either. That's why some people are leaders. They should not just tell us what to do. They should do it first.

Most of the time Moses had been a good leader. But this one special time he was not. God had to punish him, just as Moses had punished his people when they did not obey God and did wrong things.

Slowly Moses walked up to the top of the mountain. There God spoke to him.

"The land that you see is the Promised Land," God told Moses. "It is the land I promised to your people. You can look at it. But you cannot go into it."

Moses looked down at the beautiful land. He wanted to go into it. But he could not.

Now Moses wished he had done things God's way instead of his way. Don't you think that's a good idea for all of us?

WHAT DO YOU THINK?
What this story teaches: When we do things our way instead of the right way, we cannot go back and change them. Leaders must do things the right way if they expect their people to do that too.
1. Why did God punish Moses? How did he punish him?
2. Why was it so bad for Moses to do something his own way instead of God's way?
3. Why was it worse for Moses to do something his own way than for one of his people to do it?

Little Engine's Wild Ride

A Muffin Make-believe Story

Everyone liked to ride the Toyland Express. It really didn't go anywhere special, just around and around the Toyland track. But it was such fun to get on board and listen to the whistle blow.

With a chug or two, Little Engine was off, pulling the train cars behind it. Little Engine made happy sounds as it went around and around Toyland. All the toys thought the choo-choo sounds were fun.

At first, Little Engine thought they were fun, too. That's because the Toyland toys liked to ride so much. Since they liked it, they came every day. Sometimes they told Little Engine to take them around and around many times.

"Listen to Little Engine's happy sounds," said one of the toys. The others smiled and listened. They thought his sounds were happy sounds, too.

But today Little Engine was not happy. "I'm tired of pulling these cars around the track," he said. "I'm tired of pulling all these silly, laughing toys all day. I want to do what *I* want to do."

As soon as he said that, Little Engine left the track. Of course, all the train cars left the track too. They had to go wherever he went. At first, Little Engine headed down Main Street. Just think how surprised the toys were when they saw the Toyland Express coming down the street. For a while, the toys riding in the train thought it was fun. But when Little Engine almost ran over a wooden soldier and knocked Nutcracker on his side, the toys began to shout.

"Get back on the track," they shouted. "That's where you're supposed to be."

Little Engine snorted and huffed and told the toys that he was doing what *he* wanted to do. If they didn't like it, they could get out and walk.

Of course they couldn't do that. They had to go wherever Little Engine went. Before long, Little Engine was headed down the road away from Toyland.

"Stop, stop!" the toys shouted. "Get back on the track where you're supposed to be."

But Little Engine would not stop. He kept on going. Before long he came to a little pond by the side of the road. He did not know about ponds. All he had ever seen was Toyland and his track.

Little Engine headed straight for the pond. "Stop, stop!" the toys all shouted. But he would not stop. Before he knew what had happened, his two front wheels were stuck in the pond. He couldn't go anywhere now.

"Well, you wanted to do what *you* wanted to do," said one of the toys. "Now look what you have done."

"I'm sorry," said Little Engine. "Doing what I wanted to do got us all in trouble. Please help me."

All the toys got out. They pushed and shoved. Before long, Little Engine and the train cars were out of their mess. And before long they were going around and around the Toyland track.

Never after that did Little Engine leave the track. Now he wanted to do what he *should* do, not just what he wanted to do.

LET'S TALK ABOUT THIS

What this story teaches: Do you ever want to do what you want to do instead of what you should do? Be careful! You may get yourself and others into trouble.

1. Why did Little Engine leave the track and go out of Toyland? How did that get him into trouble?

2. Is it wrong to do anything that we want to do? Of course not. Then why is it wrong to do what we want instead of what we should?

3. Think of some things you should do for God or your parents. How would you get into trouble if you do what you want instead?

Better than the Best
2 Kings 2:1-11

"Elijah is the greatest," people would say. "He is the greatest prophet in Israel!"

That was true. There wasn't a greater prophet in all the land.

Elijah called down fire from heaven. He raised a boy from the dead. And he told the wicked king and queen what they were doing wrong. No one else could do all those things.

But Elijah was getting older. Who would do his work when he died? Surely no prophet could ever be as great as Elijah.

God had already arranged for another prophet to do Elijah's work when he was gone. He had sent a young man named Elisha to work with him.

Elisha went wherever Elijah went. He worked with him and prayed with him. He became more and more the kind of person Elijah was. It soon became clear that Elisha would some day do Elijah's work for him. But when? And would he be as great as Elijah? How could he hope to be greater?

One day Elisha knew that Elijah would soon leave this earth. He knew also that he should not let Elijah out of his sight. He must be there when Elijah left.

Elijah had other plans. "I must go to Bethel," said Elijah. "Why don't you stay here?"

"No, I will go to Bethel with you," Elisha answered.

At Bethel, Elisha saw some other prophets. "Do you know that Elijah will go to heaven today?" they asked Elisha.

"Of course," said Elisha. "But let's not talk about it."

Before long Elijah said to Elisha, "I must go to Jericho. Why don't you stay here?"

"No, I will go to Jericho with you," Elisha answered.

At Jericho, Elisha saw some more prophets. "Do you know that Elijah will go to heaven today?" they asked Elisha.

"Of course," said Elisha. "But let's not talk about it."

A third time Elijah tried to get away from Elisha. "I have to cross over the Jordan River," he said. "Why don't you stay here?"

"No, I will not leave you," said Elisha.

Elijah struck the Jordan River with his cloak, and the water parted. The two men walked across the dry riverbed.

"I am about to leave," said Elijah. "What can I do for you before I go?"

"I want to do greater work for God than you have done," said Elisha. "I want to have twice as much of God's power."

"That's a lot to ask," said Elijah. "But if you see me when I leave, then you will get what you ask."

Not long after that a chariot of fire came down from heaven, pulled by horses of fire. It came between Elijah and Elisha. Then Elisha saw Elijah swept up into heaven with a whirlwind. Elijah was going up into heaven without dying.

Elisha knew now that his request had been given to him. He would be greater than the greatest of all prophets. He would have twice as much of God's power as Elijah had. But Elisha would use it all to please God and to work for Him.

WHAT DO YOU THINK?
What this story teaches: Someone can become better than the best.
1. Who was the greatest prophet at first? What kinds of things did Elijah do?
2. Why do you think Elisha wanted to be greater than Elijah? Why did he want twice as much of God's power? What would he do with it?
3. What should we do with more power or more strength or more of anything if God gives it to us?

A Special Special Parade for a Special Special Person

A Muffin Make-believe Story

"Let's have a parade," said a wooden soldier. As you know, wooden soldiers like to march. And all the other toys in Toyland like to watch them.

"Why?" asked another wooden soldier.

"Because," said the first.

"That's a good reason," said the second. "But we really should have a better one. We should do it on a special day or for a special person."

The wooden soldiers thought about that for a long time. They couldn't think of a special day coming soon. And they weren't sure which special person was special enough.

"Who is more special than the king?" the first wooden soldier asked at last. "We should have the parade for him."

The other wooden soldiers could not think of anyone more special. So they all set out to see the king. They would ask him if anyone was more special.

Of course the king could not think of anyone more special. But then he didn't think about it very long either.

"I suppose you will just have to have the parade for me," said the king. He even chuckled a little.

The wooden soldiers supposed they would too. Especially since the king said so.

"Sound the trumpets," said the wooden soldier captain.

The wooden soldier trumpet players tooted on their trumpets.

"Beat the drums," the captain shouted.

You should have heard those drums!

"Raise the flag!" the captain ordered.

Someone started to raise the flag. He gave it a big tug. But the flag would not move. He gave it a bigger tug. Suddenly the rope snapped from his hands and went flying to the top of the flagpole.

The flag raiser went to look for the royal ladder. But someone had borrowed it and hadn't put it back.

"What will we do?" the king moaned.

"We can't have a parade without the flag," said the captain.

"Who can raise the flag now?" the king asked.

"I can't," said Nutcracker. Neither could any other toy in Toyland, it seemed.

"I can't either," said the king.

The toys looked at one another. They needed someone special, even more special than the king.

57

Just then the toys heard a squeak. They all turned to
see what it was. They were surprised to see the windup toy mouse headed for the flagpole. They were even
more surprised to see him go up to the top of the pole,
take the rope end in his mouth, and come down. Then
Mouse kept right on going. As he did, the flag went to
the top of the flagpole.

"Hooray for Mouse!" the king shouted. "We'll have
a special parade for him. We'll even have a special
special parade for this special special mouse."

"Hooray, hooray!" everyone shouted. Wouldn't you
like to have seen that special special parade?

LET'S TALK ABOUT THIS

What this story teaches: Sometimes we "little people" are more important than "big important people."

1. Why couldn't the parade start? Who helped it start?

2. Why was Mouse more important in starting the parade than the king?

3. Think of some important things you can do for your family. What important things can you do for Jesus?

Tales About Two Coins

What Should We Do with Money?

Matthew 22:15-22; Mark 12:13-17; Luke 20:20-25

Jesus healed sick people. He raised people from the dead. He taught and helped and did many things for others. How those people loved Him! All except a few. They hated Jesus.

The people who did not like Jesus were religious leaders in Israel. People thought the leaders should know about God and how to get to heaven. But they didn't. They thought it was more important to make rules and force people to keep them.

When Jesus helped people, those men thought people would follow Jesus instead of them. That made them jealous.

So the men wanted to hurt Jesus. They wanted to do something to make Him look foolish. Then the people would not follow Him. They would follow the religious leaders instead.

One day the religious leaders learned that Jesus was in the Temple. They made plans to trick Him.

"You are a great man," they said to Jesus when they found Him. That was a good way to start. Perhaps they could catch Him off guard.

"We know that You want to do what is right," they said. "Tell us what we should do. Should we pay taxes to Caesar or shouldn't we?"

It was a trick, and the men knew it. If Jesus said they should pay taxes to Caesar, the Roman ruler, the people would get angry. They hated the Roman ruler. Many did not think they should pay taxes to him. If Jesus said they should, the people would stop following Him.

But if Jesus said they should not pay taxes to Caesar, the religious rulers would have Him arrested. Caesar and his army ruled the land where Jesus lived. Nobody should say people should not pay taxes to Caesar. The Romans could throw Him into jail for saying such things.

What should Jesus say? What would you have said?

Jesus knew that they were trying to trick Him. And He knew exactly what He should do.

"Bring me a coin," He said.

Someone brought a coin. Jesus took it and looked at it closely.

"Whose picture is this on the coin?" Jesus asked. He knew, of course. But He wanted the men to say.

"Caesar's picture," they answered.

63

"You should give Caesar what belongs to him," Jesus said. "And give God what belongs to Him."

What could the men say? They didn't know how to answer Jesus. So they turned and walked away.

But Jesus was saying something important for us. We should pay taxes, of course. Our government uses the money to do its work. But we should also give money for God's work. And most of all, we should give our lives for God to use, for that is the best gift of all.

WHAT DO YOU THINK?

What this story teaches: We should pay money to help our government do its work, but we should also give money and time to help do God's work.

1. What were the men trying to do to Jesus? Why?

2. How did they try to trick Him? But what did Jesus do to make them look foolish?

3. Should we pay taxes? What should we do for God's work?

A Tale of Three Banks
A Muffin Family Story

"Poppi, what should we do?"

"What should we do about what, Maxi?"

"Well, I have three toy banks."

"I see, Maxi. One is a castle. Another is a church. And the other?"

"Oh, that's just an ordinary bank. That's where I keep the money for myself."

"And the castle?"

"That's the bank for Toyland's king. He has to have some money to run Toyland, you know."

"The church must hold money for God's work, right, Maxi?"

"Right, Poppi. Now what should we do?"

"What should we do about what, Maxi?"

"Well, I have a hundred pennies. This is Toyland money."

"I see, Maxi. There they are, stacked up in neat little piles."

"And I want to put them into the right banks, Poppi. But where should we put the hundred pennies? What should we do? Where should we put them?"

"Oh, I see now, Maxi. That's the same problem Mommi and I have with the dollars we get."

"But where should we start, Poppi?"

"Why not start with the church bank, Maxi? It's always good to start with God's work. Would you like to put ten pennies there? Then you would be giving God His part first."

"I would like that very much, Poppi. But which bank should we give to next?"

"Mommi and I don't get to choose. Our government decides that. Actually, it takes part of our money before we even get it."

"But—but that's not fair, Poppi. Doesn't that make you angry?"

"Sometimes it does, Maxi, especially when our leaders don't spend it the way we think they should. But we know we have to pay for firemen, policemen, soldiers, and all the people that run our government. If we didn't, they couldn't do their work for us."

"So Toyland's king must have part of the money, too. He must pay the wooden soldiers and others who run Toyland."

"I suppose so, Maxi."

"But how many pennies should we give, Poppi?"

"Mommi and I would have to pay about forty, Maxi."

"Then I will put forty pennies in the castle bank, too."

"How many pennies do you have left to put into your bank, Maxi?"

"Let's see, there are fifty pennies left, Poppi. So I will put them into my bank."

"This reminds me of the Bible story we read last week, Maxi. You know, the one about Jesus and Caesar's coin."

"How, Poppi?"

"Jesus said we should give some money to Caesar. He ran the government then. He said we should give some money to God. Of course that meant some was left for us to use."

"I'm glad we can keep some money, aren't you, Poppi?"

"Of course, Maxi. But we should ask God to help us spend that money wisely, too. Shouldn't we?"

"Then why don't we do that right now. OK, Poppi?"

"OK, Maxi!"

LET'S TALK ABOUT THIS

What this story teaches: We should give some money for God's work, just as we have to give some for our government to do its work. Then we should ask God to help us spend the rest wisely.

1. What were the three toy banks? How did Maxi divide his money among them?

2. Do you give some money to God each week? Do you ask God to help you spend what you have left?

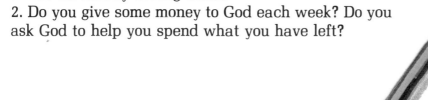

How Much Did You Give?

Mark 12:41-44; Luke 21:1-4

Jesus and His friends often went to God's house together. Sometimes they prayed. Sometimes Jesus told others about God. Sometimes they just talked with each other.

When Jesus and His friends came to the Temple, God's house, they went through a large doorway. Then they went into a wide courtyard with a stone floor. Everyone met there to talk. Some bought birds and animals from men who had set up little booths.

Moneychangers shouted to those who passed by, trying to attract attention. Foreign money could not be used in God's house, so they wanted to trade the right money for it. Of course, they charged extra to do that. Most of the time they charged too much.

Jesus and His friends walked on through that courtyard into a smaller one. Here it was quiet. No one sold birds or animals. No one shouted or traded money. This was the place where people gave their money.

68

Along the wall were strange looking boxes. Each had a lid that looked like a curved horn, with an opening at the top. People put money through the opening, just as you put money into a basket or plate at your church. That money was used to take care of God's house.

Jesus sat down by the wall, across from those boxes. He watched as people came in and dropped their offerings through the openings.

Jesus' friends watched too. They had not watched long before a rich man came in with some gold coins. He dropped some of them into an offering box.

That was a lot of money. Gold coins were valuable. Only a rich man could give that much.

Then another rich man came in. He dropped in even more coins than the first. A third rich man came in, and he gave more than either of the others.

At last a poor widow came in. She did not seem important to Jesus' friends now. They had seen the rich men give all that money. They hardly looked at the poor woman.

The woman quickly dropped in two small copper coins. They were called mites. They were not worth much.

"Who gave the most money?" Jesus asked.

His friends were surprised. Hadn't He seen that last rich man? He had dropped in more coins than anyone.

"The poor widow gave the most," Jesus said, before His friends could answer.

Now Jesus' friends were surprised. How could He say that? Surely He had seen how little she gave and how much the others gave.

"The rich man gave extra money that he did not need," Jesus said. "But this poor woman gave all the money she had."

Jesus' friends looked at each other. Jesus was right. Anyone can give extra money. But it takes a special person to give all the money he has.

WHAT DO YOU THINK?
What this story teaches: How much you give is not as important as how much you *should* give but don't.
1. Did the rich men give a lot of money? Did they give more than they kept?
2. Did the poor woman give a lot of money? Did she give more than she kept?
3. Who gave more? Why do you say that?

Building an Alphablock Tower

A Muffin Make-believe Story

Do you know what an alphablock tower is? Perhaps you have built one. All the toys in Toyland decided one day they would build one. And they wanted it to be the tallest alphablock tower ever built in Toyland.

"Bring your alphabet blocks to the Toyland gate," a wooden soldier announced. "Bring all you can. We must make this the tallest tower ever."

Can you imagine what it was like that day? Here was a wooden soldier carrying an alphabet block on his shoulder. There was another wooden soldier pulling alphabet blocks in a little red wagon. And there was another pushing alphabet blocks in a little wheelbarrow.

One by one, the blocks were put on top of each other. Before long, a wooden soldier had to get a ladder. Soon another wooden soldier had to get an even taller ladder.

"We need more alphabet blocks," said the soldier at the top of the tall ladder. "This is still not the tallest tower ever."

But all the wooden soldiers had given their alphabet blocks. Jack-in-the-Box had given all he wanted to give. So had the china doll and Nutcracker.

Suddenly trumpets tooted and soldiers stood at attention. "The king! The king!" shouted some of the toys.

71

Everyone looked toward the castle. Here came the king. He was sitting on a wagon loaded with alphabet blocks. It was pulled by toy horses.

"Look at all those blocks," a wooden soldier whispered. "That will make the tallest tower ever."

Everyone watched as the king pulled up to the tower. He gave the command, and soldiers began unloading blocks.

"One," whispered some soldiers. "Two, three, four, five . . ."

Then they stopped counting. That's because the king stopped unloading blocks. He gave the command, and the wagon loaded with blocks headed back to the castle.

"Five?" asked some of the soldiers. "He could have given half his wagon load and still have many left."

"We need three more blocks," the wooden soldier at the top of the ladder shouted. "Then we will have the tallest tower ever."

"But where will we ever get three more?" a soldier asked. "We've each given almost half of what we have."

"Except the king," whispered one soldier.

Just then someone pointed to the gate and shouted, "Look, it's Mouse!"

Everyone looked. Here came the windup mouse, pushing a little wheelbarrow. It had three blocks on it.

"Three?" said Nutcracker. "But that's ALL Mouse has."

One by one, the blocks were unloaded. One by one they were carried up the ladder. Then a shout went up. "Hooray, hooray," the soldiers shouted. "We've built the tallest alphablock tower ever. Thank you, Mouse."

Do you know who gave the most blocks? Was it the king? He gave five, but he had many left. Was it the soldiers? They gave one or two, but they gave only half of what they had. Or was it Mouse, who gave all that he had? What do you think?

LET'S TALK ABOUT THIS

What this story teaches: How much you give may not be as important as how much you keep.

1. How many blocks did each soldier give? How many did they keep? How many did the king give? How many did he keep?

2. How many blocks did Mouse give? How many did he keep? Why do you think he really gave the most?

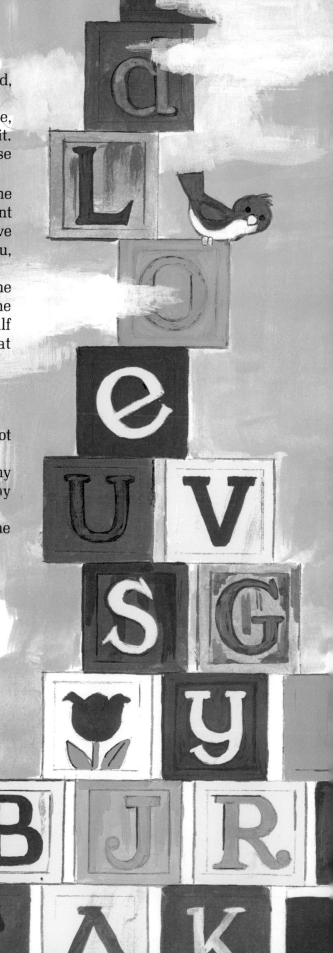

Don't Hurt Him!

Who Are My Friends?

Matthew 27:2, 11-14; Mark 15:1-5; Luke 23:1; John 18:28-38

Have you ever had a friend who wasn't a friend when you needed him? That's what happened to Jesus.

The religious leaders should have been Jesus' best friends. They said they were God's friends. They told people that they knew God. They pretended that they knew how to get to heaven.

Then Jesus came. He was God's Son. Those men should have been glad to see Him. They should have become His friends. But they didn't. Instead, they became jealous and angry. They wanted the people to listen to them instead of to Jesus.

Those men became so jealous and angry that they wanted to kill Jesus. They began to look for a way to do that without getting into trouble.

One night Jesus went into a garden to pray. The men heard that He was there. They sent some men to capture Him. They brought Jesus into a big room where Jesus' enemies, who should have been His friends, were waiting.

The men who should have been Jesus' friends asked Him many questions. They were not trying to find the truth about Him or about God. They were trying to find something wrong. They wanted to hurt Him.

At last the men stopped. They could find nothing wrong with Jesus. They would have to make up some lies. So they took Jesus to the Roman governor, a man named Pilate. It was very early in the morning, but Pilate came out of his house to talk with them.

"What do you have against this man?" Pilate asked.

"He is a criminal," the men lied.

"Why don't you judge Him?" Pilate asked.

"We can't," they said. "The law will not allow us to put a man to death. And we want Him to die."

The Romans were in charge at that time. Pilate was one of them. That's why he was governor. Only Pilate and his men could put someone to death.

"This man is a criminal," the men argued. "He is trying to be king. Your king would not like that."

When Pilate heard that, he took Jesus inside. "Are You really king of the Jews?" he asked.

"Do you want to know, or are you asking Me for someone else?" Jesus answered.

"Look, Your own people brought You here," Pilate argued. "What have You done?"

Jesus had not done anything wrong. The religious leaders knew that.

"I am a king," Jesus told Pilate. "But My kingdom is not here on this earth. If it were, the people of My kingdom would be here fighting for Me."

"So You are a king?" Pilate answered.

"Yes, I am," said Jesus. "I was born so that I could be a king, to tell people the truth."

Pilate looked surprised. He could order soldiers to kill men with their swords. He had a lot of power. But Jesus was talking about power greater than swords. Pilate was nervous and afraid of this power. Now he could see that Jesus was more than an ordinary man.

"I find nothing wrong with this man," Pilate told the religious leaders.

But they began to yell and make quite a fuss. While they did, Jesus said nothing.

How strange that was. These people were trying to have Him killed. They should have been His friends. But they weren't, were they?

WHAT DO YOU THINK?
What this story teaches: Those who should be our friends are not always our friends.
1. Who should have been Jesus' true friends? Why?
2. What did the people try to do to Jesus? Why did they do that? What would you like to have said to them?

Maxi Muffin Visits Toyland

A Muffin Make-believe Story

Don't ask me how, but one day Maxi Muffin actually got into Toyland. Jack-in-the-Box was glad to see him and jumped out of his box and smiled at him. The china doll smiled her prettiest smile and told him to say hello to Maxi. Even the Nutcracker was glad to see Maxi. He showed Maxi how he cracked nuts but warned Maxi that he should not try to do it that way too.

News spread fast, and soon almost all the toys in Toyland had come to welcome Maxi. They danced around him and made quite a lot of noise.

But not everyone was glad to see him. The captain of the wooden soldiers began to grumble.

"Look at all the fuss the toys are making over that big people thing," he complained. "They don't make that much fuss over us!"

Before long the captain of the wooden soldiers began to get all the other wooden soldiers stirred up. They began to complain about Maxi and about the way the other toys were coming to see him.

"We must get that people thing out of here," the captain told the other wooden soldiers. Maxi had never been called "that people thing" before, especially by a wooden soldier.

The captain went to see the king. "There's a big people thing that has come into Toyland," he complained. "He is making quite a fuss. If we don't stop him, he will soon be king of Toyland and you won't be!"

That got the king of Toyland excited, which is exactly what the captain wanted.

"Get him out of here," the king shouted.

The captain of the wooden soldiers smiled. Then he went to the wooden soldiers and gave orders to attack the big people thing.

"Roll out the cannons," shouted the captain. "Attack!"

Soon an army of wooden soldiers marched toward Maxi. They rolled out the cannons and loaded them with marbles and bubble-gum balls.

"Fire!" shouted the captain.

You should have seen those marbles and bubble-gum balls fly. Poor Maxi. He just wanted to be friends. He just wanted to tell all the toys how much he and Mini loved them. But the wooden soldiers wouldn't listen. They were jealous. All they wanted to do was to get Maxi, that big people thing, out of there.

Maxi could have stepped on the wooden soldiers and squashed them. He could have taken his hand and knocked them all across the room. But he didn't because he still loved them and wanted to be their friend.

So what could poor Maxi do? He got out of Toyland the same way he got in. Nobody but Maxi knows quite how he did that, but he did.

All the other toys were sad to see Maxi go. But the wooden soldiers weren't. They had been too jealous to see that Maxi was really their best friend. Don't you think they did a foolish thing?

LET'S TALK ABOUT THIS

What this story teaches: Those who should be good friends sometimes turn against us and try to hurt us.

1. How do you know that Maxi wanted to be a friend in Toyland? Why didn't the wooden soldiers let him be a friend to them?

2. Have you ever had friends turn against you? How did you feel?

3. The religious leaders should have been Jesus' friends. They said they loved God. They said they were God's helpers. So they should have welcomed God's Son. But they didn't. Do you know why?

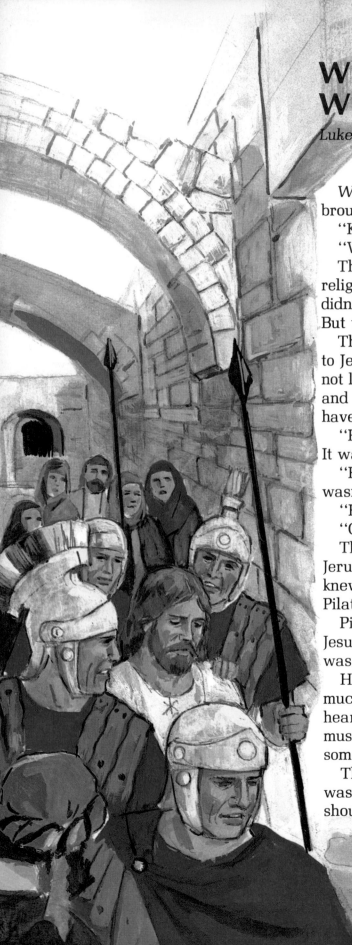

What Should I Do?
What Should I Say?

Luke 23:6-12

What should I do? Pilate wondered. Some men had brought Jesus to him.

"Kill Him!" the men argued.

"Why?" Pilate asked.

The men should have been Jesus' friends. They were religious leaders. They pretended to love God. But they didn't. They pretended to help people get to heaven. But they didn't.

The men were jealous. They saw many people listen to Jesus. They saw many people follow Him. They did not like that. They wanted the people to listen to them and follow them instead. That is why they wanted to have Jesus killed.

"He tells people not to pay their taxes," they argued. It wasn't true. But it made Pilate nervous.

"He causes riots," the people told Pilate. That wasn't true either. But Pilate did not know what to say.

"He stirs up trouble in Galilee," the men shouted.

"Galilee?" asked Pilate. "Is He from Galilee?"

That gave Pilate an idea. Herod was visiting here in Jerusalem. Herod was ruler of Galilee. Now Pilate knew what he would do. He would send Jesus to Herod. Pilate would not have to kill Jesus. Herod could do it.

Pilate called for some Roman soldiers. They took Jesus through the streets to the house where Herod was staying.

Herod was delighted to see Jesus. He had heard much about Jesus but had never met Him. He had heard much about Jesus' miracles and thought they must be magic tricks. He thought it would be fun to see someone do magic tricks.

The soldiers took Jesus to the room where Herod was sitting. Jesus' enemies came too. They began to shout terrible things about Jesus.

"What should I say?" That's what you or I would have asked if we had been Jesus. But Jesus didn't say anything.

Then Herod began to ask Jesus questions. He kept on asking question after question.

"What should I say?" That's what you or I would have asked if Herod had been talking to us. But Jesus didn't say anything.

At last Herod grew tired of asking Jesus questions. He and his soldiers began to make fun of Him. They put a king's robe on Him. Then they laughed and pretended that He was a king.

But still Jesus said nothing. He did not even get angry. Before long Herod and his soldiers gave up. How can you fight a man who never gets angry? How can you argue with someone who never talks back?

Herod did not know what to do with Jesus. So he sent Him back to Pilate.

Jesus could have called an army of angels down to destroy Herod. But He didn't. What did He do? Nothing. What did He say? Nothing. How can you fight or argue with that?

WHAT DO YOU THINK?
What this story teaches: There are times when it is better to be quiet and not get angry or fight back.
1. What were Jesus' enemies trying to do to Him?
2. Did Jesus get angry and fight back? What did He do instead?
3. What did Herod and his soldiers do to Jesus?
4. Did Jesus get angry and fight back at them? What did He do instead?

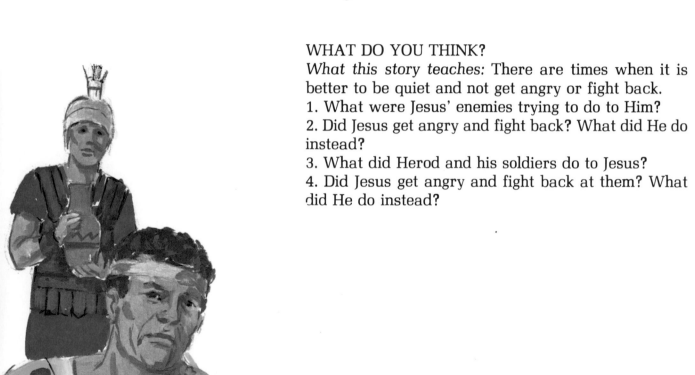

What Should I Do?

A Muffin Family Story

What should I do? Maxi wondered.

Maxi stared at the wooden soldiers on his bedroom floor. They looked like any other wooden soldiers now. But when Maxi had gone to Toyland, these wooden soldiers had become jealous. They did not like all the attention Maxi got from the other toys. So they chased Maxi out.

But now Maxi was here in his bedroom. And now the wooden soldiers were just toy wooden soldiers.

Maxi knew he could stuff the wooden soldiers in a box and put them on a shelf. He could even throw them into the garbage can. Or he could step on them and make a terrible mess of them.

What should I do? Maxi wondered. He wanted to talk with someone. But he couldn't talk with Mini. She would wonder how he got into Toyland. He couldn't talk with his friends either, or with Mommi or Poppi. Nobody would think he really went to Toyland.

Maxi wanted to talk to Jack-in-the-Box. But Jack couldn't answer now. Toys can't talk unless you are with them in Toyland. So, of course, Maxi could not talk with the china doll, the windup mouse, or Nutcracker. He couldn't even talk with the wooden soldiers to see if they still felt jealous.

Maxi decided he would sit down to read and think about what he should do. So he picked up a book called *Toyland Tales*. Maxi liked to read Muffin Family books because they were about him and his family.

Do you know what story Maxi found? It was the Bible story about Jesus, when people took Him to Herod. The people were trying to hurt Jesus, just as the wooden soldiers had tried to hurt Maxi. Herod even made fun of Jesus. So what did Jesus do? Maxi wondered what he would have done if he had been Jesus.

When Maxi read the rest of the story, he found out what Jesus did.

Jesus could have asked angels to come down and squash Herod. But He didn't. He could have zapped Herod with a bolt of lightning. But He didn't. He could have told Herod what a bad man he was. But Jesus didn't even do that.

Do you know what Jesus did to Herod? He didn't do anything. He didn't even talk back to Herod or argue with him.

Now Maxi knew what he should do. He would not talk back to the wooden soldiers. He would not squash them or put them in a box on a shelf. He would just forgive them and play with them.

Sometime I will try to go back to Toyland and become friends with them, Maxi thought. *But now I will just forget what they did.*

Before long, Maxi was happily playing with his wooden soldiers on the bedroom floor. Don't you think Maxi did what he should?

LET'S TALK ABOUT THIS

What this story teaches: Sometimes it is better not to argue or fight back. Sometimes it is better to keep quiet.

1. What had the wooden soldiers done to Maxi when he visited Toyland? Why had they done that?

2. What could Maxi have done to the wooden soldiers? Why didn't he?

3. What did Maxi learn from the Bible story? Have you ever kept quiet when you could have fought back? What happened?

Don't Listen to Them!

Matthew 27:15-16; Mark 15:6-15; Luke 23:13-25; John 18:39—19:16

Pilate was worried and confused. He didn't know what to do.

Jesus' enemies had brought Him to Pilate. They had said some terrible things about Jesus. They wanted Pilate to put Jesus to death.

Pilate knew that Jesus had not done those terrible things. He did not want to put Him to death. Why should he? So he sent Jesus to Herod. He hoped Herod would do something with Jesus. If he did, Pilate would not get into trouble.

But Herod did not want to get into trouble either. So he sent Jesus back to Pilate. Now here was Jesus again. And here were Jesus' enemies again, shouting and fussing and arguing. What should he do?

Then Pilate had an idea. "Each year you ask me to let one prisoner go," Pilate told Jesus' enemies. "Should I let Jesus go?"

"No," they answered. "Let Barabbas go instead."

Pilate was surprised. Barabbas had killed a man. He should stay in prison. He should not go free.

Then Jesus' enemies began to stir up the crowd. People began to shout at Pilate to let Barabbas go.

"But what shall I do with Jesus?" Pilate asked.

"Crucify Him! Crucify Him!" the people shouted.

Pilate was even more worried now. While all this was going on, his wife sent a message. "Leave Jesus alone," she said. "He has done nothing wrong. I had a bad dream about Him."

Pilate decided that he would make the people feel sorry for Jesus. So he sent Jesus away to be whipped. Soldiers took a whip with pieces of metal at the end and beat Jesus until it tore His skin. Then they pushed a crown of thorns over His head.

Pilate's men put a purple robe on Jesus. Kings wore purple robes. But the soldiers were doing this to make fun of Jesus.

The soldiers laughed and pretended to bow down to Jesus. Then they slapped Him in the face.

While Jesus was bleeding from His cuts, Pilate brought Him out before the people. Surely now they would feel sorry for Him. They would ask Pilate to let Him go. But they didn't.

"Crucify Him! Crucify Him!" they shouted.

"You do it." Pilate demanded. "I find nothing wrong with Him."

"Our law says He must die," the people shouted. "He says He is God's Son. Anyone who says that should die."

That frightened Pilate. So he took Jesus into his palace to talk with Him.

"Where are you from?" he asked Jesus. But Jesus said nothing.

"Don't you know I have power to put you to death or set you free?" Pilate said.

"You have no power over me except the power that God gives you," Jesus answered. "But those other people are sinning even worse than you."

Now Pilate was even more sure that Jesus should be set free. But the people outside said no.

"You are not Caesar's friend if you let this man go," they shouted. Caesar was the emperor, the man over Pilate. He could put Pilate to death.

"He is your king," Pilate argued.

But the people kept on shouting, "Crucify Him!" Crucify Him!" By this time, the crowd was getting noisy. If this kept up, they could start a riot.

90

At last Pilate gave up. He would have Jesus crucified. But he wanted some way to show that he did not want to do it.

Pilate brought a basin of water. He washed his hands in front of the crowd. "I do not want to be punished for this," Pilate told the people. "You are to blame."

"If anyone is punished, it will be us and our children," the people shouted back.

So Pilate let Barabbas go. Then he sent Jesus away to be crucified. Pilate should not have listened to those people. But he did.

WHAT DO YOU THINK?
What this story teaches: Don't listen to the wrong people. They will get you into trouble.
1. What did the people in the crowd want Pilate to do? Why should he not have done that?
2. Why then did Pilate give in to them? What should he have told them?
3. What would you like to say to Pilate?

How Do I Get Home?
A Muffin Make-believe Story

"Will you come with me to Toyland, Mini?" Maxi Muffin asked one day.

Mini thought Maxi was teasing at first. But when he showed her how easy it was to pretend his way there, she decided it would be fun to go.

So before you could say "Toyland," Maxi and Mini were there. Jack-in-the-Box jumped out of his box to say hello. He was glad to see Maxi again. So were the china doll and Nutcracker. And of course the windup mouse came racing up to see Maxi and Mini.

"I wonder if the wooden soldiers will try to chase us out?" said Maxi. Just then the captain of the wooden soldiers saw Maxi. He came running up and bowed down before Maxi.

"Please forgive me," he said to Maxi. "I know now that you want to be our friend. Jack and Nutcracker told us so. I'm sorry for what we did to you before."

Of course Maxi forgave the wooden soldiers. So they wanted to do something to show Maxi and Mini that they were their friends now.

The wooden soldiers started a parade for Maxi and Mini. They marched through the gates and down the streets. They even took Maxi and Mini to see the king.

At last the parade was over, and it was time to go home. But Maxi had forgotten how to leave Toyland and go back to his house.

"Here are some tops," said Maxi. "They really look busy going around and around. I will ask them."

"Do what we're doing," said the tops. But when Maxi and Mini whirled around and around like the tops they did not go home. They just became very dizzy instead.

"Look, there's a merry-go-around," said Mini. "Let's ask the horses. Perhaps they can take us home."

"Jump on and we'll get you there," said the horses. But they didn't. They just kept going around and around.

"Oh, dear," said Mini. "I'm afraid we will never find our way home."

"We'll get you there," said the wooden soldiers. They started another parade. They marched up one street and down another street. But they never did get Maxi and Mini home.

Maxi and Mini sat down in the middle of Toyland. They felt so sad. Maxi was beginning to think he would not find his way home either.

"Why so sad?" a voice asked. Maxi and Mini looked up. There was Nutcracker.

"We can't find our way home," said Maxi.

"Well, how did you get here?" asked Nutcracker.

"Oh, that was easy," said Maxi. "I just imagined that we were coming and there we were." Then Maxi jumped up. Now he remembered. He would get home the same way he had got to Toyland.

"Thank you, Nutcracker, thank you." Maxi called.

But before Nutcracker could answer, Maxi and Mini were safely home. It was a good idea to ask the right person, wasn't it?

And it wasn't such a good idea to ask the ones who didn't know.

LET'S TALK ABOUT THIS

What this story teaches: Listening to the wrong people can get you into trouble. It pays to listen to someone who knows.

1. Why couldn't the tops help Maxi and Mini find their way home? Why couldn't the merry-go-round horses?

2. Who did help Maxi and Mini. How did he help?

3. Do you remember the Bible story about Pilate and Jesus? Pilate listened to the wrong people. Who were they? How did that cause him to do the wrong thing?

4. Have you ever listened to the wrong people? What did they want you to do? Why should you not listen to people who try to get you to do wrong things?

5. What should you do when people try to get you to do wrong things? Will you remember next time?

Mini's Word List

Twelve words that all Minis and Maxis want to know:

ANCESTORS—These were fathers and mothers, grandfathers and grandmothers, great-grand-fathers and great-grandmothers, and so on.

CAMEL—This animal was a favorite with people who had to travel across a desert on a long trip. Camels could carry hundreds of pounds. They could go for several days without water.

CAVE—Bible-time people sometimes buried their family and friends in caves. Abraham buried Sarah in a cave.

COINS—During most of Old Testament times, people did not have coins. But people in Jesus' time had them. Most coins were made of gold, silver, or bronze.

CRUCIFY—Jesus was crucified. He was nailed to a cross with the nails going through His hands and feet. That was a way Romans put people to death.

GOVERNOR—Pilate was a governor when Jesus was on earth. The ruler over him was the emperor, who was like a king. Pilate ruled over a small area, something like a county today.

HORN—Some trumpets were made of silver. Others were made of large seashells. Still others were made of animal horns. Animal horns were also used like jars to hold olive oil. The offering boxes in the Temple, God's house in Jesus' time, were shaped like horns.

SCALES—Scales were called balances. A rock or piece of metal was put on one side. People knew how much it weighed. Something to be weighed was put on the other side.

SILVER—In New Testament times, gold and silver were made into coins. But in Old Testament times people weighed bars or pieces of gold or silver jewelry. They used pieces of gold or silver for money.

SOLDIERS—Men who fought in armies were called soldiers. They had to do what kings wanted them to do.

TENT—In Bible times many people lived in tents. Some people moved from place to place with their animals, so the animals could get fresh grass. It was easy to move a tent, but of course they could not move a house.

WHIP—Jesus was beaten with a whip. It was sometimes called a scourge. Sharp pieces of lead were put at the ends. They cut deep into a person's skin.